Gymnastics Jean

Written By Jeanna M. Zivalich

Illustrated By Abira Das

Books may be purchased by contacting Amazon at www.amazon.com/dp/1500946702, (206) 508-4051 or www.jeannazivalichbooks.com, (312) 533-8228.

Published by: Jeanna M. Zivalich
Interior Design by: Abira Das, Calcutta, India
Cover Design by: Abira Das, Dark Hues
Editing by: Diana Mucci-Beauchamp

ISBN-13:978-1500946708
ISBN-10:1500946702
First Edition
Printed in United States of America

Dedication

Gymnastics Jean is dedicated to every child reading this book.
If you desire to do something healthy and fun in school, like joining
a team; you'll need steady practice. If you practice hard and stay
focused, you have a better chance at being successful and reaching
your goal.
Don't give up. I'm rooting for you!

J ean awoke in the morning
all keen and excited.
It was gymnastic tryouts,
and she was delighted.
She hopped out of bed,
brushed her teeth and her hair.
And by then smells of breakfast
were filling the air.

Searching for her prettiest
pink dress to wear to school,
she found the cute flowered
one that looked really cool.
Running down the hall with her
book bag on her back,
she passed the kitchen counter
grabbing her lunch and snack.

"Good morning everyone.
Breakfast smells good!" Jean said.
As she sat to eat her eggs,
bacon and toasted bread.
Mom said, "You're so cheerful
and look fantastic."
Jean replied, "Today is tryouts
to join gymnastics!"

"We have been practicing
every day now for two weeks.
And our coach is teaching us
a lot of new techniques.
I am trying out to join
team Twirling Queens.
And my friend Lynn is trying
out for the Jumping Beans."

Sarah now noticed the school bus
coming down their street,
so she called out to Jean
to hurry up and eat.
Jean finished, and they kissed
Mom and Dad goodbye.
Hand-in-hand they both
walked to the school bus nearby.

Jean daydreamt in class about joining Team Twirling Queens, and her best friend Lynn would be joining Team Jumping Beans. Oh, the fun they would have practicing twirls and flips, and both teams would compete for the championship!

Tryouts began. Jean felt
anxious and a little scared.
She jumped on the balance beam
as her classmates just stared.
Gracefully she was
walking across the beam.
Thinking how great it will
be when she joins the team.

Now it was time for the
final leap-off, twirl and flip.
She felt sweat begin to
gather on her fingertips.
The moment she waited
for was finally here.
She began to hear the sounds
of the small crowd cheer.

She ran and leapt off of the
beam like a fast rocket.
Something went wrong, and she
fell on the padded carpet.
It was so quiet you could
hear a pin drop.
Jean knew her audition
tryout was a flop.

Her Coach said, "Don't worry,
I'll help you along the way.
Just keep practicing a
little bit every day.
Giving up will not get you
where you want to be.
You become good at something
by practice, you see."

Now it was Lynn's turn to leap off of the balance beam. She dreamt of one day joining the Jumping Bean's Team. She leapt off of the beam like a fast rocket, and landed on her feet on the padded carpet.

JUMPING BEANS

Classmates cheered and
lifted up Lynn praising her success.
Lynn asked her coach, "Can I join?"
And the answer was yes!
Jean was sad because she did
not make the team.
All because she fell when she
leapt off of the beam.

Coach took Jean aside and
told her never to give up.
She said, "With steady practice
you will catch up.
You can try out again
to join the team.
You'll do better, so keep
focused on your dream."

Jean learned if there is a
team you want to join in school;
practice and never give up.
It's the number one rule.
"You can do it. Keep practicing."
her coach always said.
Her words of support
were remembered in Jean's head.

Jean tried out again the
next season to join the team.
She practiced, never gave up,
and now is a Twirling Queen!

Author's Published Work
Jeanna Zivalich Books are available in English and Spanish
www.jeannazivalichbooks.com

Dean wakes up the morning of November 9 with excitement and anticipation. It's his birthday today! He is 3 years old. He is so full of excitement on this special day that he wakes up and shouts with a loud voice, "Hey, it's my birthday today!" Little does Dean know what Mommy and Daddy have in store for him today when he is given his special birthday gift surprise!

Dean se despierta la mañana del 9 de noviembre. Cumple sus tres años de edad. Se despierta con una explosión de energía, estusiasmo y muchos deseos de gritarle al mundo:"¡Es mi cumpleaños hoy!". Además, el pequeño Dean sabía en donde, mamá y papá, tenían guardo su regalo de cumpleañossorpresa.

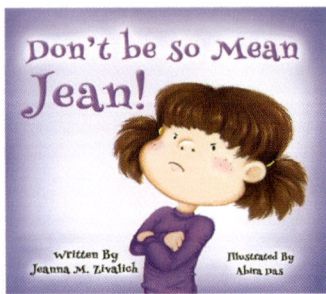

Jean is a 7 year old girl who plans a day of fun outside in her back yard. Going outside to play was the only thing on her mind. But each time she attempts to head out to play, Mom asks her to first make her bed and do her homework. After Jeans finished with each of mom's requests of things to do, she thinks she will get to go outside to play. But mom changes Jeans plan and decides she should go upstairs and play with her little sister Sarah instead. Jean was not happy about the change of plans and her attitude will show it. Jean will soon realize that being mean and unkind to her sister Sarah was wrong.

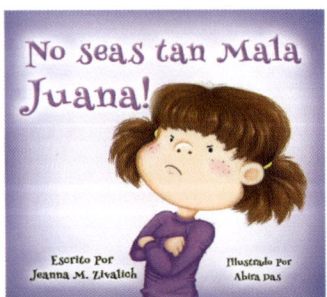

Juana es una niña de 7 años quien planea un día de diversión afuera en su jardín. Salir a jugar era la única cosa en su mente. Pero cada vez de que ella trataba de salir a jugar, mamá le pedía que primero tendiera su cama e hiciera su tarea. Después de que Juana término con cada una de las cosas que su mamá le pidió, piensa ella que va poder salir a jugar. Pero mamá cambia los planes de Juana y decide que sería mejor que subiera a jugar con su hermanita Sara. Juana no le gusto el cambio de planes y su actitud lo demostró. Juana pronto se dará cuenta que ser mala y cruel con su hermana Sara esta incorrecto.

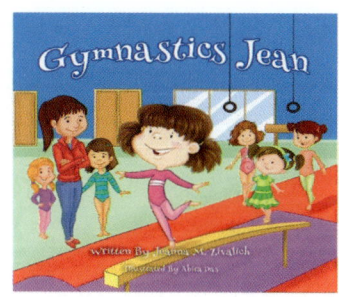

Jean is a 7 year old girl who loves gymnastics. She loves to twirl, flip, and walk on the balance beam. Jean dreamt of joining the Twirling Queen's Team at school one day. On the morning of tryouts she was so excited and was sure to do well that day; but during tryouts something went terribly wrong and Jean was faced with a big disappointment. She did not make the team. With the help of her coach, practice, positive encouragement and support, Jean overcame her temporary set back. She never gave up and tried out again the next season and because of her hard work and practice, she did so well she was able to join the Twirling Queen's Team.

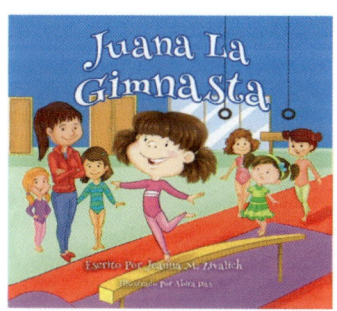

Juana es una niña de 7 años quien quería ser parte del equipo de gimnasia de su escuela. Durante la audición paso algo terrible y Juana tuvo que enfrentar una decepción. Con la ayuda de su entrenadora, estímulo positivo, y apoyo, Juana supero su atraso y nunca perdió esperanza de poder un día ser parte del equipo Las Pequeñas Reinas Piruetas.

Upcoming Next Release
A Children's Bible Story about Creation

Printed in Great
Britain
by Amazon